WHEN I GROW UP

By Judy Ainsworth

Photographs by Belinda Durrie

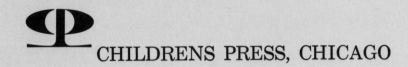
CHILDRENS PRESS, CHICAGO

*For Gray and his friends who appear in this book,
and also for Sharron, Cassandra, Zoraya, and Todd*

Library of Congress Catalog Card Number: 69-14686

WHEN I GROW UP

87590

Once there was
a little boy.
He asked his mother
the same question
every morning.
"Am I a man yet,
Mommy?"
"Not yet, dear. Eat
your breakfast," his
mother would answer.

"I want to be a man,"
said the little boy.
"Why are you in
a hurry to grow up?"
asked his mother.
"Because it is fun
to be a man. When I grow
up, I can stay up late
at night."

"I can go to work."
"Good-bye, dear. See you tonight."

"When I grow up
I can work in my
office."

"I can drive a car.
I can take my children
for a ride in the country."

"When I am a man
I can be big and strong
like Daddy."

"Why can't I be a man now, Mommy?"

"Because you are not ready," said Mother.

The little boy thought about this for a while.

Then he went to talk to his daddy.

"I want to be a man,"
said the little boy.
"Someday you will
be a man," said Daddy.
"But I want to be a
man now," said the boy.
"It is fun to be a man."

"It is a fine thing to be grown up," said Daddy. "But I remember how much fun it was to be a boy. Sometimes I wish I were a boy again."

"Really?" said the boy.

"Yes," said Daddy. "I remember how much fun it was to run through a field. Sometimes I found something wonderful–

like a climbing tree,
big enough for everyone."

"I can remember spending all day building a secret hideout, when I was a boy," said Daddy.

"When you are a boy," said Daddy, "you always can play pretend games.

"You can talk about secret plans, like what you are going to do tomorrow."

"When you are a boy, tomorrow is always filled with suprises. Like finding a perfect spot to play marbles. Oh yes," said Daddy, "it is fun to be a boy."

That night when Daddy
came to kiss him goodnight,
the little boy said:

"Daddy, I think I will
be a little boy for a few
more days."

"That's fine," said
Daddy. "There is plenty
of time to be a man."

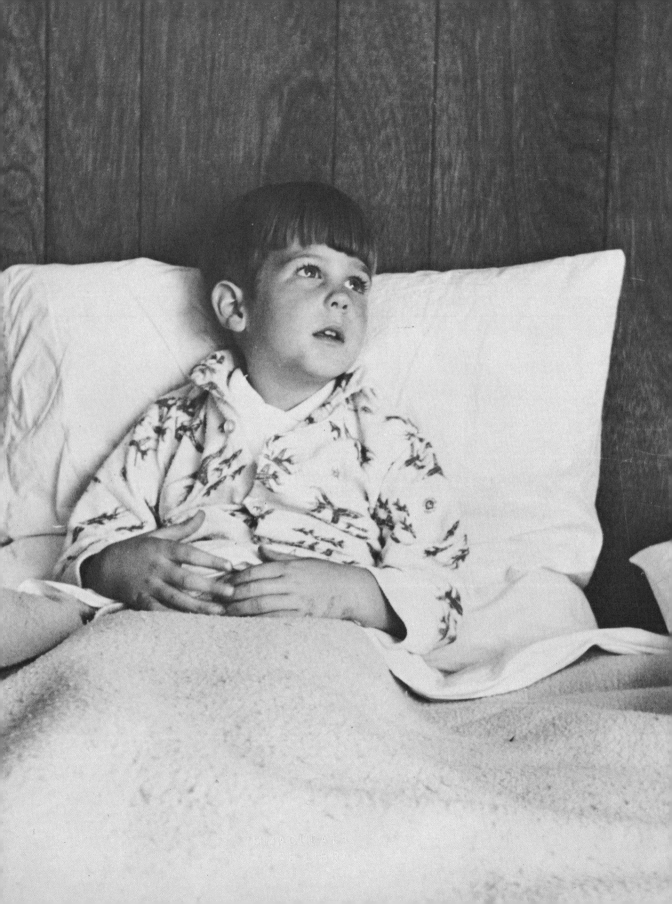